TIME FOR KIDS

Good for Me
Love

Sharon Coan

Publishing Credits

Rachelle Cracchiolo, M.S.Ed., *Publisher*
Conni Medina, M.A.Ed., *Managing Editor*
Jamey Acosta, *Content Director*
Dona Herweck Rice, *Series Developer*
Robin Erickson, *Multimedia Designer*

Image Credits: Cover, p.1 ©iStock.com/naphtalina; p.3 ©IStock.com/Monkey Business Images; p.4 ©iStock.com/woogies1; p.5 ©MBI/Alamy; p.6 ©iStock.com/Whitney Lewis Photography; p.8 ©iStock.com/Sakdawut Tangtongsap; p.9 ©iStock.com/Martinan; p.10, 12 ©iStock.com/EVAfotografie; all other images from Shutterstock.

Library of Congress Cataloging-in-Publication Data

Coan, Sharon, author.
Good for me : love / Sharon Coan.
pages cm
Summary: "Who do you love? This book shows how we share our love."— Provided by publisher.
Audience: K to grade 3.
ISBN 978-1-4938-2153-2 (pbk.)
1. Interpersonal relations—Juvenile literature.
2. Helping behavior—Juvenile literature.
3. Conduct of life—Juvenile literature. I. Title. II. Title: Love.
HM1146.C625 2016
152.4›1—dc23

2015015023

Teacher Created Materials
5301 Oceanus Drive
Huntington Beach, CA 92649-1030
http://www.tcmpub.com

ISBN 978-1-4938-2153-2

Printed by: 51497
Printed in: China

I love you.

I love you.

You love me.

I love you.

You love me.

I love you.

You love me.

I love you.

You love me.

Words to Know

love